Fantastic Four

THE IMAGINATION RING

by Brent Sudduth
Illustrated by Mangaworx

Meredith® Books
Des Moines, Iowa

ISBN 0-696-22508-5

The Mayor wanted to honor the Fantastic Four at an awards ceremony. The four were getting ready to go to City Hall. Mr. Fantastic, Invisible Woman, Thing, and . . . wait a minute! Where's Human Torch?

"Flame-head's late again!" yelled Thing, as he climbed into the Fantasticar.

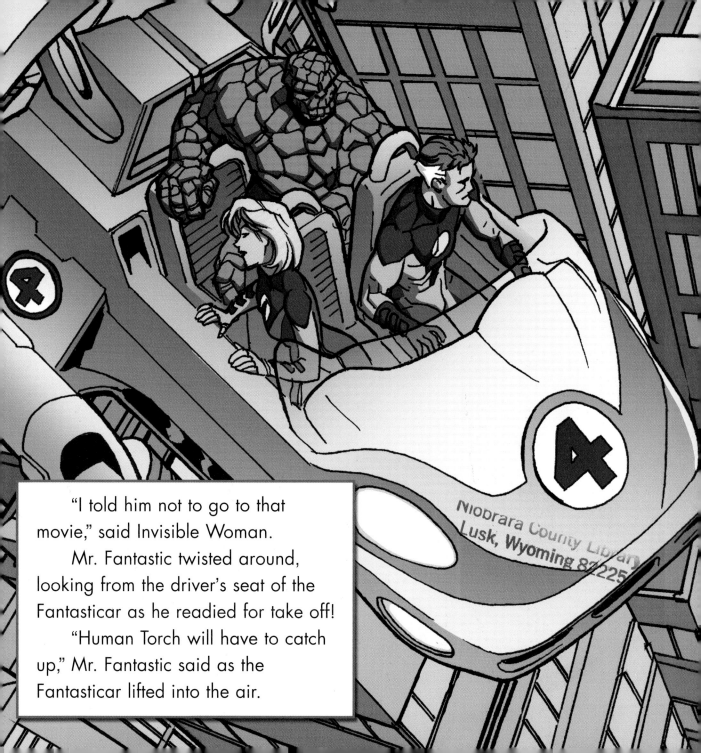

"I told him not to go to that movie," said Invisible Woman.

Mr. Fantastic twisted around, looking from the driver's seat of the Fantasticar as he readied for take off!

"Human Torch will have to catch up," Mr. Fantastic said as the Fantasticar lifted into the air.

"What a great movie!" Human Torch shouted as he entered the Fantastic Four's headquarters. He quickly looked around and saw that no one was home.

"Where is everyone?" he called out just as he saw the Fantasticar speed away. "There they are, and here I go!"

"Flame on!" shouted Torch as he blasted off to catch up. His entire body burst into flames as he rocketed skyward.

"'Bout time you caught up, Flame-head!" barked Thing. "What's the matter? Couldn't find your way home?"

Torch flew alongside the Fantasticar, confused as to where everyone was headed.

"What's the rush?" he asked Invisible Woman.

"I told you not to go to that movie. Now you've made us late for the awards ceremony," lectured Invisible Woman.

"Sorry, Sis, but it really was a great movie!" Torch explained.

"Hang on, I'm bringing us in for a landing," Mr. Fantastic said. "There's City Hall now!"

City Hall, the Mayor, and hundreds of fans awaited the arrival of the Fantastic Four.

The Mayor greeted the Fantastic Four with a big smile. "Welcome to Hero Awards Day. We want to give you just what you deserve," said the Mayor.

"Thank you, Mr. Mayor," said Mr. Fantastic. Just as he was about to say more, the Mayor began to shake, rumble, and glow.

"Are you OK, Mayor?" asked Invisible Woman.

Right before their eyes, the Mayor began to change!

"Wonderful to see you all," said a strangely familiar voice that came from the now-changed Mayor.

"That voice! I'd know it anywhere," said Mr. Fantastic, as he stretched to get away from an evil he knew all too well.

"Yes, Mr. Fantastic, it is I—Dr. Doom!" said the voice. "Look around and see how happy your fans are to see you."

The Fantastic Four spun around to see that all the fans were now Doom Bots! "What do we do? We're surrounded!" whispered Invisible Woman as the Doom Bots inched closer.

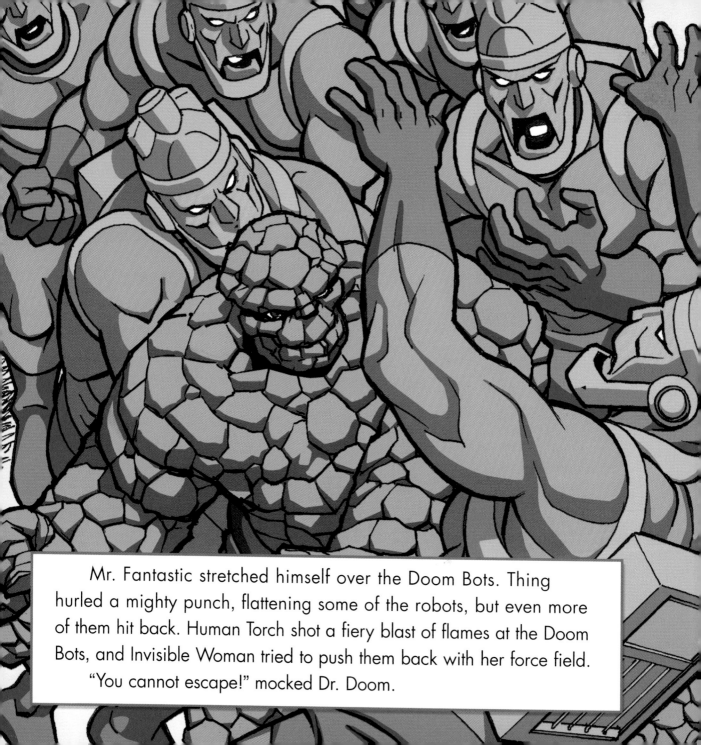

Mr. Fantastic stretched himself over the Doom Bots. Thing hurled a mighty punch, flattening some of the robots, but even more of them hit back. Human Torch shot a fiery blast of flames at the Doom Bots, and Invisible Woman tried to push them back with her force field.

"You cannot escape!" mocked Dr. Doom.

Gas erupted from the hands of the Doom Bots, and the Fantastic Four fell unconscious.

"What a revoltin' dilemma this iszzzzzzzzz…," said Thing as he fell. The Doom Bots grabbed the heroes and carried them into the sky!

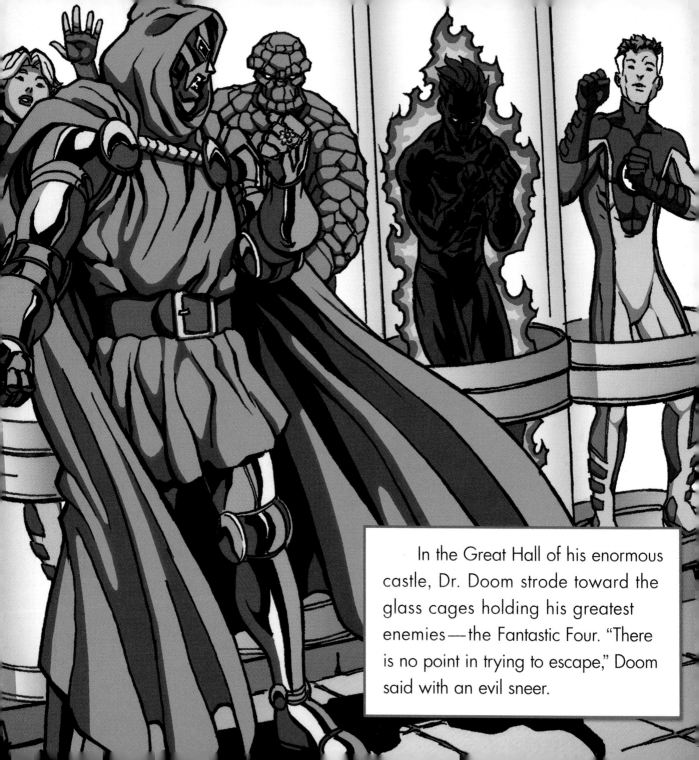

In the Great Hall of his enormous castle, Dr. Doom strode toward the glass cages holding his greatest enemies—the Fantastic Four. "There is no point in trying to escape," Doom said with an evil sneer.

"You have finally failed, Mr. Fantastic, and I am here to see that you know it. You are the one who caused the destruction of my very first experiment, and yet everyone thinks you are a genius. But I know the truth," seethed Doom.

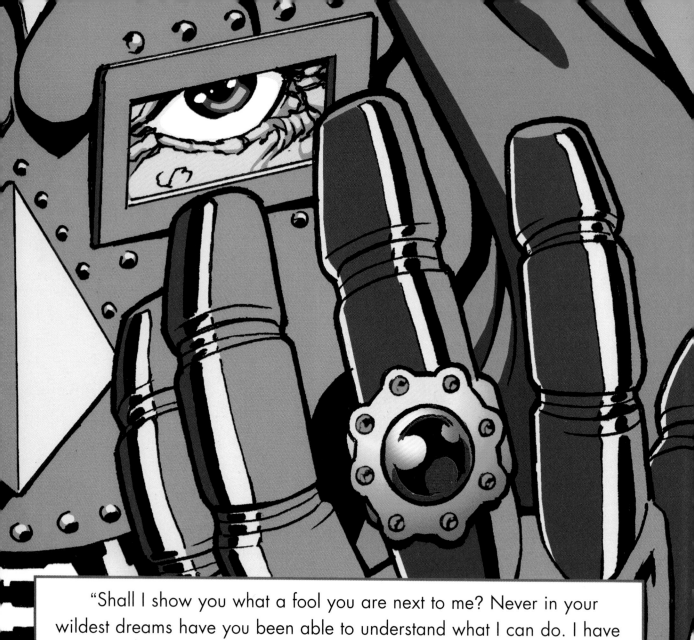

"Shall I show you what a fool you are next to me? Never in your wildest dreams have you been able to understand what I can do. I have created the greatest weapon ever—the Imagination Ring!" roared Doom. The ring glowed as Doom taunted the four.

"What is that?" asked Human Torch.

"Looks like a bubble gum ring to me, Metal-face!" Thing said, as he banged on his cell walls.

"Doom, you know that ring is dangerous," said Mr. Fantastic. "You can't use it!"

"With this ring, anything I imagine comes true. If I think of food," said Doom as the ring glowed, "then it's mine." Instantly, a pile of food appeared. "Or see that cat? I prefer it larger," he said, and the cat turned into a lion!

"No Doom, your own bad decisions caused your first experiment to explode. That ring is no different! Be careful! It's dangerous!" pleaded Mr. Fantastic.

"Enough!" commanded Dr. Doom. "It is time for you to feel my awesome power!"

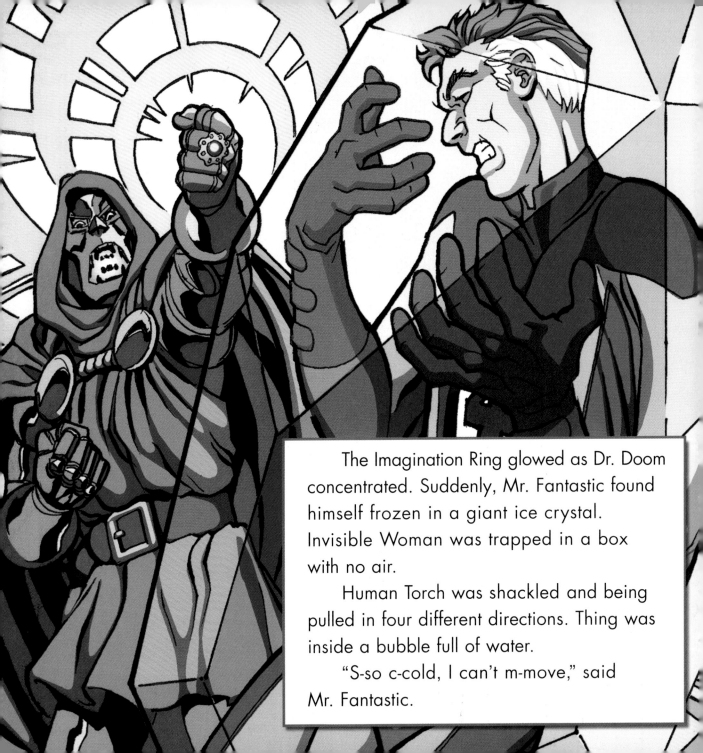

The Imagination Ring glowed as Dr. Doom concentrated. Suddenly, Mr. Fantastic found himself frozen in a giant ice crystal. Invisible Woman was trapped in a box with no air.

Human Torch was shackled and being pulled in four different directions. Thing was inside a bubble full of water.

"S-so c-cold, I can't m-move," said Mr. Fantastic.

"I'm running out of air!" screamed Invisible Woman.

"I can't burn these shackles off! I'm being pulled apart," yelled Torch.

No matter how hard he hit, Thing was stuck underwater and couldn't breathe!

"I can't help myself, but I can help someone else," Torch grunted. He shot flames, bursting the ice crystal holding Mr. Fantastic.

Mr. Fantastic slithered into a tiny opening and expanded himself inside the box holding Invisible Woman until it broke open.

"Stop resisting!" commanded Dr. Doom, as the Imagination Ring began to shake and spark.

Invisible Woman extended her force field into the water around Thing, giving him badly needed air. Thing took a breath and tore Torch free of his shackles. Then Torch returned the favor as he burned off Thing's water bubble.

"Blast you, Fantastic Four, you overloaded the ring when you fought back! I can't control it," screeched Doom. The ring glowed as Dr. Doom yelled, "This isn't over—," and he was gone.

"Where do you think Dr. Doom went?" asked Torch.

"I'd guess he's in the last place he was imagining," said Mr. Fantastic.

Dr. Doom sat trapped in one of his own cells. "I'll be back, Fantastic Four," he yelled to the stone walls.